BBC Children's Books
Published by the Penguin Group
Penguin Books Ltd, 80 Strand, London, WC2R 0RL, England
Penguin Group (USA) Inc., 375 Hudson Street, New York 10014, USA
Penguin Group (Australia), 707 Collins Street, Melbourne, Victoria 3008, Australia
Penguin Group (NZ), 67 Apollo Drive, Rosedale, Auckland 0632, New Zealand
Canada, India, South Africa
Published by BBC Children's Books, 2014
Text and design © Children's Character Books
Illustrations by Jorge Santillan
004

Contents

When *is* the Doctor?

The TARDIS takes the Doctor on his travels through space and time, never knowing where or when it will end up next. Sometimes the Doctor is able to choose where he is going, but frequently the TARDIS decides for him, transporting him into the far future or way back in time to the very beginnings of the universe itself.

But something very strange is going on. No matter what time period the Doctor finds himself in, things are not as they should be. The boundaries of time are blurring, mummies lurk in the shadows at the Ancient Greek Olympics, cavemen visit Aztec temples, and aliens are appearing everywhere...

Spotter's List

The following things can be found in every scene:

The Doctor	The TARDIS	Amy Pond	Rory Williams

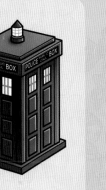

ANCIENT EGYPT

Watch out for mummies as you walk like an Egyptian through this scene to find the Doctor and his friends.

SHACKLETON'S EXPEDITION

Join Ernest Shackleton aboard *The Endurance* in 1915 and search the Antarctic for the chilly Time Lord and his companions.

NEW EARTH

Travel to the year 5,000,000,023 to track down the Time Lord.

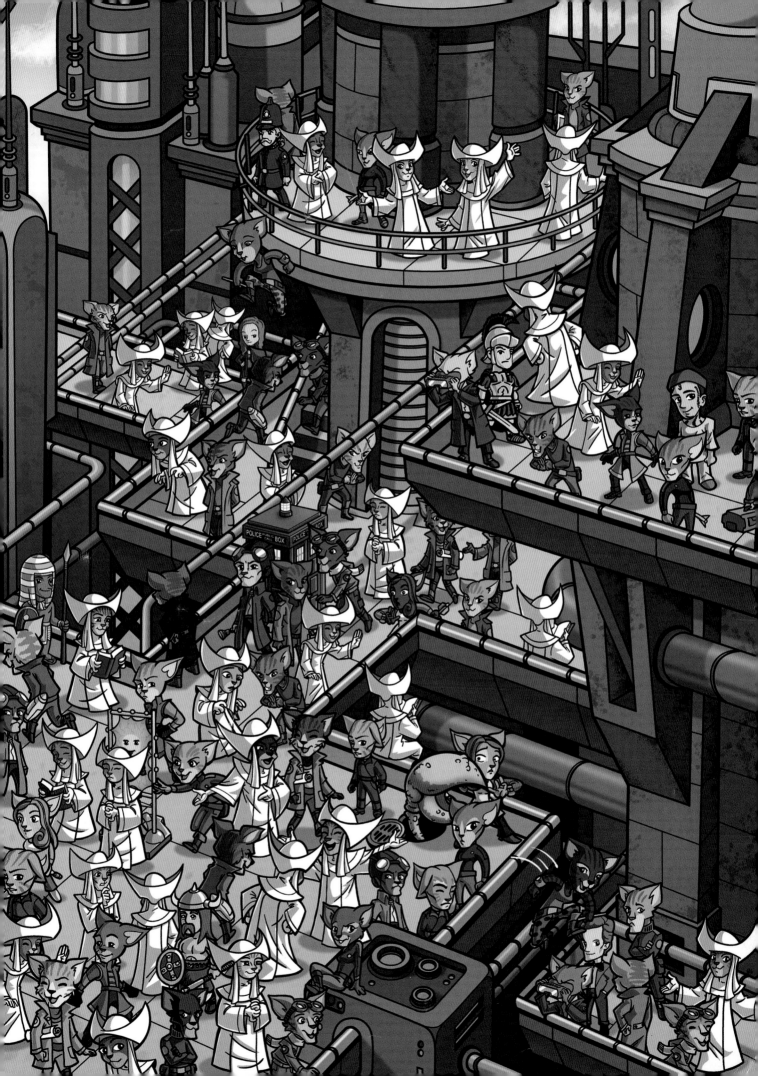

ANCIENT ROME

Roam Ancient Rome and look out for
Rory Williams, the Lone Centurion,
Amy Pond and the Doctor.

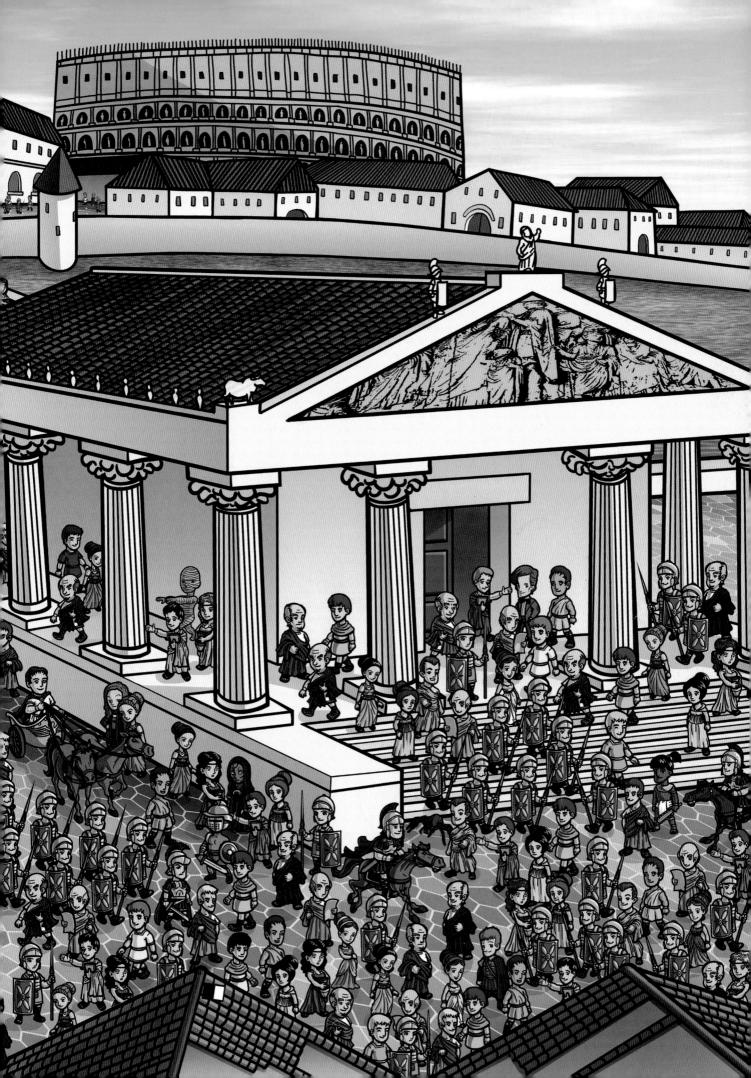

THE STONE AGE

Have a rocking time as you seek out the
TARDIS and those who travel in her.

VICTORIAN LONDON

Fly back to 1851 to walk the streets of
Victorian London and find the Doctor
and his friends.

THE END OF THE WORLD

Travel to the year 5.5/Apple/26 in the far future and search Platform One for the Doctor, Amy and Rory before the Earth gets roasted!

ANCIENT GREEK OLYMPICS

Keep your head down and beware of javelins flying through the air as you search the very first Olympics in 776BC.

TARDIS GRAVEYARD

Journey to another time and another universe to find the Doctor, Amy and Rory… and the only complete TARDIS among the debris!

THE VIKINGS

It's back to the 11th century, so beware rampaging Vikings... not to mention terrifying creatures lurking beneath the sea!

METEBELIS III

Travel hundreds of years into the future to a distant planet ruled by giant spiders! Can you find the Time Lord and his friends before the monsters do?

THE AZTECS

Go back to 15th-century Mexico and track down the Doctor and his friends before they're all sacrificed to the Aztec rain god!

ST JOHN'S MONASTERY

There's a double for everyone to be found in this 22nd-century Ganger factory, including the Doctor and his companions...

More to find...

Ancient Egypt page 8

- [ ] A green book
- [ ] An Egyptian with a mohican
- [ ] A Pyrovile
- [ ] A knight in shining armour
- [ ] A tyre
- [ ] A purple mummy
- [ ] A Roman helmet
- [ ] One of the Sybilline Sisterhood
- [ ] A pair of glasses
- [ ] A violin
- [ ] Ten differences between the Hieroglyphics on the columns

One of the Sybilline Sisterhood

A Pyrovile

A Yeti

A TARDIS road sign

Shackleton's Expedition page 10

- [ ] A boom box
- [ ] A mummy
- [ ] A clown
- [ ] A TARDIS road sign
- [ ] A Yeti
- [ ] An astronaut
- [ ] A white Dalek
- [ ] A pocket watch
- [ ] A Roman Centurion
- [ ] A snowman
- [ ] A Cybershade
- [ ] K-9

New Earth page 12

- [ ] A cat with a ball of wool
- [ ] A policeman
- [ ] A Roman soldier
- [ ] A Viking
- [ ] An Ancient Greek
- [ ] A caveman
- [ ] The Face of Boe
- [ ] Claw of the Macra
- [ ] Cassandra
- [ ] An Egyptian
- [ ] A seal
- [ ] Chip

A cat with a ball of wool

Chip

ANCIENT ROME page 14

- ☐ A policeman
- ☐ Cassandra
- ☐ The Pandorica
- ☐ A Pyrovile
- ☐ A mummy
- ☐ The Psychic Paper
- ☐ A penguin
- ☐ An Aztec
- ☐ A Sycorax
- ☐ A giant spider
- ☐ The High Priestess of the Sybilline Sisterhood

A Sycorax

A Mummy

A Scarecrow

The Wooden King

THE STONE AGE page 16

- ☐ An Aztec
- ☐ A Scarecrow
- ☐ A policeman
- ☐ The Sonic Screwdriver
- ☐ A Weeping Angel
- ☐ A Roman Centurion
- ☐ A stone Dalek
- ☐ A snowman
- ☐ A Dalek cave painting
- ☐ A mummy
- ☐ The Wooden King
- ☐ A Yeti

VICTORIAN ENGLAND page 18

- ☐ Fourteen cats
- ☐ Miss Hartigan
- ☐ A Cybershade
- ☐ Queen Victoria
- ☐ Jackson Lake – The Next Doctor
- ☐ Charles Dickens
- ☐ A Stone Age man
- ☐ A Slitheen
- ☐ A werewolf
- ☐ A Cyberman
- ☐ A clown
- ☐ A Cat person

Queen Victoria

A Slitheen

Moxx of Balhoon

Steward

THE END OF THE WORLD page 20

- ☐ Moxx of Balhoon
- ☐ Face of Boe
- ☐ Ten Metal Spiders
- ☐ A Slitheen
- ☐ Cassandra
- ☐ Steward
- ☐ A cat with a ball of wool
- ☐ The Heavenly Host
- ☐ A pocket watch
- ☐ The Sonic Screwdriver
- ☐ The High Priestess of the Sybilline Sisterhood

ANCIENT GREEK OLYMPICS page 22

- [ ] A caveman
- [ ] Prisoner Zero
- [ ] An Aztec
- [ ] A Minotaur
- [ ] A Cyberman
- [ ] K-9
- [ ] The Sonic Screwdriver
- [ ] A penguin
- [ ] The Olympic torch
- [ ] A mummy
- [ ] The Isolus
- [ ] The Heavenly Host

A Minotaur

K-9

Idris

A Winder

TARDIS GRAVEYARD page 24

- [ ] Idris
- [ ] A Winder
- [ ] An Ood with Green Eyes
- [ ] Davros
- [ ] A Handbot
- [ ] A Krillitane
- [ ] A Catwoman
- [ ] A penguin
- [ ] A Roman soldier
- [ ] An Aztec
- [ ] K-9
- [ ] A Toclafane

THE VIKINGS page 26

- [ ] A Sea Devil
- [ ] The Flood Monster
- [ ] Vampire of Venice
- [ ] Two Peg Dolls
- [ ] A Catwoman
- [ ] Werewolf
- [ ] A yellow Dalek
- [ ] Slitheen
- [ ] A policeman
- [ ] A Roman
- [ ] A Minotaur
- [ ] A Scarecrow

A Sea Devil

The Flood Monster

A Toclafane

A Judoon

METEBELIS III page 28

THE AZTECS page 30

A Silurian

The Heavenly Host

Doctor Ganger

An Adipose

ST JOHN'S MONASTERY page 32